Who knows where and when children begin to dream? But dreams are what life is (or should be) about. Harry, despite his humble circumstances and with the support of his family, is able to dream.

This story is written by a real chocolate maker, Mark Tarner, president of The South Bend Chocolate Company. Mark's company grew from his dreams. There's a little bit of Harry in Mark. The chocolate factory is real, as are the streets.

This place could be anywhere, but it does exist in a mix of reality and fantasy. Harry's dream is in all of us if we look closely enough. South Bend's neighborhoods are made of dreams. It's an everyday magical place that Harry gives us a glimpse of. It's a place we all know.

Harry's
Sweet Dream

Written by - Mark Tarner
Illustrated by - Terri Christie

ISBN # 0-9729364-0-8

To Julie, Emily, Sam and Anna.
In your hearts my love has found a home.

Special thanks to Maria and Christina.
Without your effort this book would not have been possible.

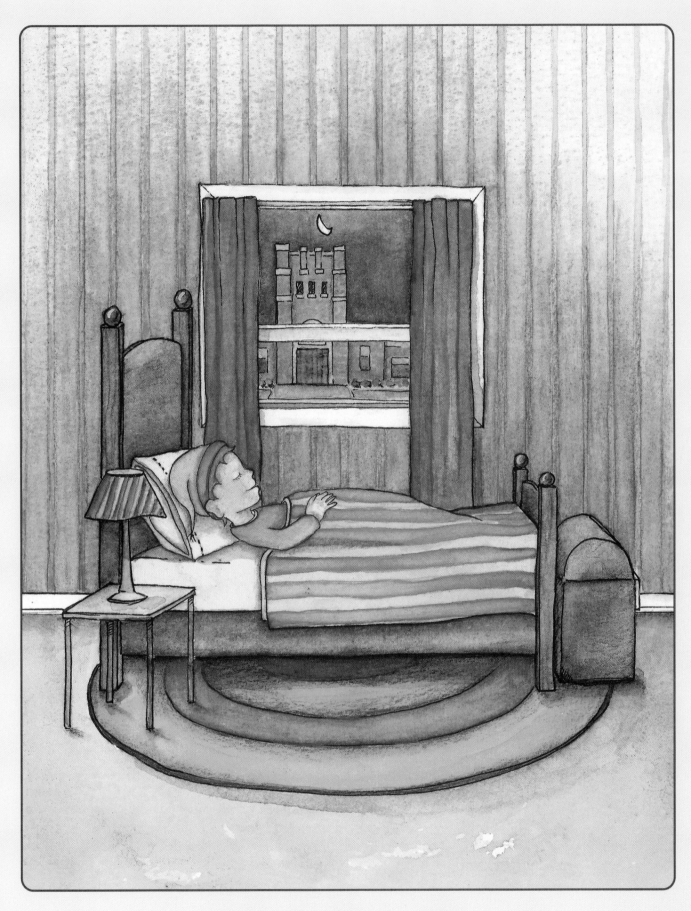

Harry had a dream. . .

Harry dreamed of
working at the chocolate factory
at the end of the street.

Harry told. . .

. . .no one.

Harry had a sister named Harriet --
Harriet Harrison.

Harriet knew Harry had a dream.
Harriet told no one.

Harry and Harriet lived on Lake Street
in a small house with their parents,
Hal and Hortense Harrison.

Hal worked at a factory.
Not the chocolate factory.
All the fathers in the neighborhood
worked at factories.

Hortense worked at a hairdresser.
She knew everyone in the neighborhood
and loved to talk and was a great cook.
Hortense worked on the same street as the
chocolate factory-on Sample Street.

Harry wanted to be like his dad and
Harriet wanted to be just like her mom.
They loved when dad came home and
they all ate Hortense's fabulous dinners.

Harry always wanted chocolate for dessert.
He could close his eyes and smell it in the air.

Every so often, Mr. Harrison came home from work
early and Mrs. Harrison made dinner a little early.
Without saying a word, Harry and Harriet knew. . .

. . . .that the Harrisons were off to the
chocolate factory.

Down Lake Street and across Sample Street.
The short walk always seemed longer than it was.

Today,
Harry would share his dream.

Harry's heart raced
as his dad opened the big metal doors.

Then it sank! How did Harry think he could
work at the chocolate factory when he wasn't
even big enough to open the front doors?

Harry froze.

"Come along Harry, they're about to close,"
Hortense whispered in Harry's ear as she
guided him to the factory store.

The store was a magical place. Cases filled with chocolates, ice creams and many kinds of sodas, gifts and trinkets! And old chocolate boxes!

After he ordered a chocolate milkshake,
Harry tried to count the old boxes -- 1-2-3-4...
8-9-10... Harry could only count to ten.
So there are tens of tens of chocolate boxes
in the store, thought Harry.

Harry's shake came. He could feel the straw
tighten as he drew the chocolate ice cream
closer to his lips. . . . Aaaah. . . .

Harry had a busy day at the chocolate factory.
He felt sleepy and climbed into his father's lap.

He was quiet for a moment then said, "One day
I want to work at the chocolate factory."

"Okay, Harry, One day, one day,"
said Mr. Harrison

The Harrisons smiled at each other
and their clerk and started home.

Sweet Dreams, Harry!

Mark Tarner is an award winning businessman, community leader, and father. Harry's Sweet Dream is his first children's book. Mr. Tarner lives in South Bend, Indiana.

Terri Christie is an Illustrator/Designer and mother of one. She lives with her husband and daughter in Northern Michigan.